How Riley Rescued the Huffy Woofer

by Dawn E. Garrott
Illustrations by Luthando Mazibuko

Bahá'í Publishing
Wilmette, Illinois

Bahá'í Publishing, 401 Greenleaf Avenue, Wilmette, Illinois 60091
Copyright © by the National Spiritual Assembly of the Bahá'ís of the United States
All rights reserved. Published 2015
Printed in Mexico on acid-free paper ∞

17   16   15   3   2

Library of Congress Cataloging-in-Publication Data

Garrott, Dawn E.
  How Riley rescued the huffy woofer / by Dawn E. Garrott ; illustrations by
Luthando Mazibuko.
      pages cm
  ISBN 978-1-61851-094-5 (alk. paper)
  1. Bahai Faith—Juvenile fiction. I. Mazibuko, Luthando, illustrator. II. Title.
  PZ7.G1866Hm 2015
  [Fic]—dc23
                              2015015647

Illustrations by Luthando Mazibuko
Book design by Patrick Falso

DEDICATION

This is dedicated to my aunt, Jeanette Kinney Cakouros
with thanks for her support and encouragement.

ACKNOWLEDGMENTS

Sincere thanks to to my husband, William Riley Garrott, whose biography this is <u>not</u>; to my uncle, John Cakouros, for his support; to my aunt, Ruth Kinney Flowers, for her interest and encouragement; to my friend, Wendy McVicker, for always being there for me and her steadfast belief in my ability to make unique contributions; and to the hardworking staff of Bahá'í Publishing for their helpfulness and perseverance.

CONTENTS

Chapter One

Lost in the Woods

Riley couldn't catch up with his brother, William. He shouted, "Wait! Mom said to stay together!" They hadn't lived in Hartland, Ohio very long, and Mom didn't want anyone to get lost.

William stopped his borrowed scooter to wait under a shady tree. Their neighbor, Jonathan, who was riding his own bicycle, stopped beside him.

"You're too little to keep up," Jonathan, who was eight, said to Riley when he joined them.

"I'm almost six," said Riley, trying to catch his breath. "How can I keep up without a bike or a scooter?"

"You can't ride a bike, anyway," said William. His voice sounded like Dad's voice. He was almost seven and he looked like Dad, too. He was tall for his age and thin, while Riley was more like Mom, short and heavy.

Riley wanted them to know that he was big enough to play with them, so he said, "I can too ride a bike." He said it so quickly that he forgot to add, "almost."

Jonathan said, "OK, here. You can ride mine."

Riley felt surprised because William wouldn't share unless Mom or Dad made him. The bike was wonderful, blue with yellow streaks of lightning. Better yet, it was smaller than the bike he and William had used while staying with Grandpa and Granny recently. Riley hoped it would be easier to ride. He had fallen several times when he had asked Grandpa to let go.

"Do you want to ride it or not?" Jonathan asked.

Riley nodded and soon was standing astride the bike. His excitement died as he realized he didn't know what to do next. If he hopped up onto the seat before the bicycle was moving, he would fall over. If he tried to run to get moving, he couldn't hop up onto the seat.

William said, "Get on. I'll push the way Grandpa did."

As Riley hopped on the bike, his brother gave him a quick shove on his back. For one glorious moment, he was riding the bike! The pedals turned with the wheels and hit his legs. When he glanced down, the bicycle wobbled toward a telephone pole. One foot found a pedal and pushed, helping him get his balance, but the pole seemed to rush at him.

"Turn!" shouted William.

"Brake it!" shouted Jonathan.

At that moment Riley couldn't remember how the brakes worked, so he turned the handlebars. Unfortunately, he turned too fast and too hard. He and the bike tumbled onto the sidewalk beside the pole.

"Ow!" he shouted, scraping his elbow and landing with a heavy thud. The fall hurt so much that he wanted to cry. However, Jonathan said that even his little sisters weren't crybabies.

As Riley climbed to his feet, he hardly noticed when his hand brushed a torn sheet of paper lying near the telephone pole. William was right—he couldn't ride the bike. Now, for sure, they wouldn't want him with them.

Suddenly, he felt very angry. No matter how much he tried, what he did wasn't good enough. He said to William in a loud, blaming voice, "You pushed me too hard!"

William said, "I did not! I was helping. You're just too little."

"I'm not too little," shouted Riley.

"You're just a big baby!" William shouted back.

They weren't allowed to hit each other, but Riley had never wanted to punch his brother more than he did right then.

Jonathan interrupted to say, "The bike is OK. Come on, let's go!" He got on it and began to roll away.

William got the scooter. "Come on!" he echoed Jonathan and scooted after him.

Riley looked at the ground to hide the angry tears that spilled down his cheeks. Why did William get to be born first? Because of that, he got to do everything first and Riley couldn't keep up. It wasn't fair!

Riley saw the piece of paper still lying on the ground by the telephone pole and picked it up. At first he only pretended to look at it as he followed the boys, but then he got interested. He realized that he was holding a torn picture of the front half of a dog. He turned and walked back to the telephone pole. Yes, the paper had come off the pole. He could tell because part of it was still dangling there, ruined by the last rain.

Rain had also messed up the writing on the piece he held. He wasn't sure if the first letter was an "l," but he could make out a blurry "o" and an "s" and a "t." So what? He couldn't read yet, either! William had learned how to read in first grade. Riley would start first grade in the fall, but that didn't help now.

Folding the tattered paper, he put it in his pocket and started after the boys again.

Except—where were they? He looked up and down the street. No boys anywhere. He hurried to the end of the block, stopped at the tall red stop sign, and looked back and forth. Still no trace of them. He wasn't allowed to cross streets alone, so he turned the corner and hurried along the sidewalk. He didn't like being alone like this.

Suddenly Riley felt homesick. All his life he had lived in Manhattan, New York City, New York. He was used to walking beside tall buildings, not houses with green lawns. He was used to wide streets filled with cars and trucks, not narrower streets with almost no one driving by. He was used to sidewalks crammed with colorful people, not sidewalks empty as far as he could see. He was used to loud city noises, not to birds singing and leaves rustling in a summer breeze. He was used to lots of smells, including yucky garbage can smells and wonderful restaurant smells. It wasn't that he didn't like the smell of flowers and mowed grass. It was that, right then, he missed what he was used to.

Riley planned to stop at the next corner to look for William and Jonathan again, but there wasn't another corner. Instead, the sidewalk ended in front of one last house. Beyond it, the street became a road that went off into the countryside between fields of tall grass.

He wished that he had his giant stuffed dog with him. But he had loaned Woofus to Grandpa and Granny to protect them from increasing crime where they lived. Woofus was big and brave and could keep anyone safe. Well, so could God. Riley knew that because God had helped him tame the invisible monster that he felt sure lived in the old house that his family had moved in to recently. He had recited a Bahá'í prayer to help solve the problem and he knew that God had answered his prayer because the monster didn't get him. He wasn't even afraid of it anymore.

Deciding that now was a good time to say the prayer again, Riley stood respectfully with his eyes closed and sang the words. He liked to sing and that made it easier to remember. "Is there any remover of difficulties save God? Say: Praised be God! He is God! All are His servants and all abide by His bidding."

His eyes flew open the second he finished because he thought he heard the boys. Yes! Surely it was their voices coming from behind the last house, where the woods began and its backyard ended.

"I'm coming," Riley yelled, and ran down the driveway beside the house, across the backyard, and into the woods. Soon he stopped and called, "Where are you?" As he looked around among the trees and undergrowth, he discovered a path wide enough for a bike and scooter to pass single file.

Coming from somewhere ahead of him, the sound repeated, a low noise like muffled laughter. He guessed that they were teasing him, so he hurried on quietly. The path grew fainter. He was thinking about how fast God had answered his prayer when he realized that the path had disappeared. He walked here and there looking for it, but he couldn't find it anywhere. When he tried to go back the way he had come, he couldn't tell which way that was. With a sinking feeling in his stomach, he realized that he was lost in the woods.

Chapter Two

WHAT RILEY DISCOVERED

"William? Jonathan?" Riley called. "Where are you?"

No one answered.

Riley wasn't angry at his brother any more. In fact, he wanted very much to see him. William would know the way back to their new old house. If Riley ever got back, he wouldn't even care that it looked like a haunted house from a Halloween cartoon.

He swallowed back a shout for help. Could it be that God was busy and hadn't heard his prayer after all? He started to repeat the prayer but, at that very moment, he again heard the sound that had drawn him into the woods. Only this time, it was much closer and he realized that it wasn't the boys at all. It was an animal.

He stood still among the trees. Did lions or tigers live in Ohio? He wasn't sure. He tried to say, "I wouldn't taste good and my sneakers wouldn't taste good, either," but the words wouldn't come out.

Again, he wished he were in Manhattan. No lions or tigers or other wild animals lived in Manhattan. Everyone knew that. They lived in the Bronx, another part of New York City. He had seen them there at the zoo. When his family had visited the zoo, they had watched as the lions were fed big chunks of raw meat, which they grabbed with sharp claws and tore apart with pointed teeth.

Whatever the thing was, it began to move around like it didn't care who heard it. Bushes swished and dried twigs snapped. Still, it huffed and snuffled in a way that no lion or tiger would. Could it be a bear with a summer cold?

Then came the sound of digging. Dirt and old rotting leaves came flying past Riley, some of it hitting his t-shirt and jeans. He didn't run away, though. Instead, he ran forward because, at that very moment, he had heard a worried whine followed by a deep "woof!"

Sure enough, the animal was a dog, but what a dog! It had a wide head and a flat nose. As soon as the dog heard Riley, it turned toward him, stopped digging, and grinned. Then its large pink tongue flopped out of its mouth and hung down between its white and black and brown cheeks. The cheeks also hung down because they had way more skin than they needed.

Riley laughed, bent down a little, and held out his hand. He knew he shouldn't go up to a strange dog, but he felt sure that this dog wouldn't hurt him. The panting animal pushed past his hand and licked his whole face. Riley laughed again and threw his arms around its short, thick neck in a big hug. He noticed two things almost at the same time. First, it was the fattest dog he had ever seen. And second, it wore a heavy collar. A chain went from the collar to a nearby tree.

Had the dog been chained there on purpose? Or had the chain simply caught around the tree? Riley studied it. Having found one end, he moved it this way and that way, trying to decide. Suddenly, it came undone and he found himself holding the chain like the end of a long leash.

"Woof!" said the dog again and charged off into the bushes, dragging Riley along behind it.

"Whoa," shouted Riley. But the dog kept pulling him, while branches hit his face and arms. The chain was hurting his hands and he knew he couldn't hold on much longer. How could he make the dog stop?

They were in a small clearing now, still moving fast. Just ahead stood a full-grown tree. With a burst of speed, Riley ran on one side of the tree while the dog ran on the other side. The chain caught around the tree and yanked them both to a halt.

"Oof!" huffed the dog.

"Ow!" cried Riley because his hands hurt even worse. In desperation, he yelled, "Sit, doggy! Sit!" To his amazement, the dog sat. Riley quickly wrapped the chain around the tree. Then he sat down, too.

After he had caught his breath, he talked to the animal, "I'm thirsty. I'm hungry. I don't know where I am. Nobody knows where I am. I want to go home and I don't know how to get there. Where do you live?"

The dog lay down, put its heavy head in Riley's lap, and sighed. It looked into his face with trusting brown eyes. It seemed to be waiting to see what he would do. Riley realized something then. As big as the dog was, it could not take care of him. He would have to take care of it. When he understood this, a strange thing happened. He forgot to be afraid any more.

Riley stroked the dog's head. Soon it fell asleep. It began to snore loud, huffy snores through its pushed-in nose. Riley wanted to laugh, but he didn't want to wake it up. He kept petting it and enjoying its doggy smell. He hoped this dog would become his own special friend. Since William and Jonathan didn't want him with them, he would play with the dog instead.

But first he had to get the dog home. He decided not to sing the Bahá'í prayer again. He guessed that God was probably like Dad. If Riley kept asking for help, Dad would say, "Try to do it yourself. You can't learn if you don't try."

So he thought for a while and came up with a plan. He would let the dog pull him some more. Sooner or later, the dog would pull him out of the woods because the woods couldn't go on forever. Then he would find someone in a uniform and ask to go home. He hoped the police officer would be on a horse, like they sometimes were in Manhattan. He liked horses, too.

Riley blew on the dog's wet, black nose and it woke up with a huge sneeze. They scrambled to their feet. Then, suddenly, Riley stood still, listening. He heard voices, and they were very, very close.

Chapter Three

THE HIDEOUT

Riley heard one voice say, "The dog has to be here." A second voice said, "This way. Follow the sneeze." Then Jonathan's sisters came into the clearing and stopped, surprised to see Riley standing there.

The girls were twins, already six years old. Although they looked alike, Riley could tell them apart. Samantha, called Sam, grinned and spoke. "William is looking for you. He said he can't ever go home if he doesn't find you. He's mad!"

"Oh," said Riley. Then he grinned back. They would know the way home because their family lived beside his new old house. Besides that, he liked them. They made things fun.

Pamela, called Pam, said, "You were supposed to stay together."

"I know," said Riley, "but I got lost when I couldn't keep up."

She said, "The dog got lost, too. We found her and hid her here."

Sam had been carrying a bowl and a bottle of water. She poured the dog a drink. It started lapping up the water before she could even set the bowl down. As she petted the thirsty dog, she said, "Look how her sides stick out. She's going to have puppies."

"Oh," said Riley. "I thought she was just fat." The twins giggled. How could he not have known that the dog was pregnant?

He asked, "Why are you hiding her? Why didn't you take her home?"

Sam answered, "Because our mother would make us give her back to her owner and Pam wants a puppy."

Pam added, "Bulldog puppies cost a lot. Our father says he doesn't have that kind of money to spend on a dog. We've saved eleven dollars and seventy-three cents, but that's not enough."

Sam agreed. "We need maybe a thousand hundred dollars and we'll be grown up before we have that much."

"So we're hiding her until her puppies are born," Pam explained. "Then we'll keep the littlest one and give the dog and all the other puppies back."

Riley asked, "Isn't that stealing?"

"Sort of," Sam admitted. "But if we keep the smallest one, then we're not stealing as much. Right?"

Riley didn't know about that. But he had another question. "What if she has the puppies here in the woods when you're gone?"

The girls looked at each other in a special way they had. It seemed like they were talking without saying a word. Then Sam said to him, "It's OK for you to know about the hideout."

"What hideout?" asked Riley.

"We'll show you," said Pam. Before Riley could even warn her about the dog pulling, she undid the chain. "Heel!" she said in a very bossy voice. Then she walked away and the dog walked beside her.

Sam picked up the bowl and, as they followed, she explained, "Pam saw a woman make a dog heel on TV. She's going to train tigers in the circus. Tigers are harder to train than dogs. I don't want scratches all over me, so I'll clean the cages."

The trees and bushes began to be more widely spaced. Soon, the girls stopped. Sam whispered to Riley, "I'll go first," and she slipped away.

Pam whispered, too, as she said, "When she gives me the signal, I'll sneak the dog in. Then, if no one is around, you come in as fast as you can."

Riley asked, "What signal? Come in where?"

Pam didn't answer because she was already running with the dog in the direction Sam had gone.

Riley hadn't heard a signal of any kind. He didn't want to be alone again, however, so he hurried after them right away. Astonished, he saw them disappear into the carriage shed in his own backyard.

Forgetting to look around to make sure that no one could see him, he rushed out of the woods.

Chapter Four

CAUGHT!

"There he is!" shouted Jonathan.

"Hey, Riley!" yelled William.

Dismayed, Riley stopped by the big tree in his family's backyard, the one the twins had been sitting in the first time he ever saw them. If he continued to the carriage shed now, the boys would find out about the dog.

"Hey," Riley called back unhappily. As the boys came toward him, he looked away, wondering what to do. That's how he noticed the narrow pieces of old wood that the girls had climbed like a ladder to get up the tree. He began to climb these, even though the rusty nails let the rotted wood move under his feet.

"Don't run away again," called William. "We've been looking for you."

Riley didn't speak until he got up to the lowest of the big branches. He sat down carefully. The boys looked smaller down below, their faces turned up toward him. He asked, "Are you mad at me?"

Jonathan stood grinning as William answered. "I was, but I'm not now. Don't tell Mom, OK? It can be our secret. Just the three of us."

Riley liked the idea of having a secret with the older boys as well as the girls. He felt important having two secrets. "OK," he said.

Jonathan said, "It's easier to go up than down. Maybe you'll have to live there."

"I can get down," Riley said. But now it seemed like a long way to the ground.

Just then, Mom came out the back door. "Boys," she called, "it's almost time for supper and we have to get ready to have Bahá'í Feast afterward. William, where's Riley?"

William pointed and said, "Up there!" at the same time Riley called, "Here I am!"

Riley felt a rush of happiness when he saw his mother standing there in her old cut-off blue jeans, her sandals, and her t-shirt with pictures of laughing children of all races. He wanted to give her a big hug. Squirming around onto his belly, he groped for the top piece of wood with one foot.

Mom started toward them from the back porch. "Be careful, Riley," she said. "Those slats are rotten."

It was when he turned his head to tell her that he was being careful that he fell. He landed on the ground with a thud that knocked all the air out of him. Before he knew it, Mom had pushed aside the boys and pulled him to his feet. As he was finally about to draw a breath, she said, "O my goodness! He isn't breathing!" She slapped him so hard on the back that he still couldn't take a breath.

"O my goodness!" she cried again. "His arm is bleeding."

"Yeah," said William. "That's from the scrape he got when he fell off . . ." A sudden sharp jab from Jonathan's elbow reminded him of the secret and he hastily stopped talking so he wouldn't say too much by mistake.

To Riley, the world seemed dark and fuzzy. He desperately needed to breathe. His mother held both his shoulders and shook him hard while she shouted, "Breathe!" in his face. But she was shaking him, so he still couldn't. Instead, he blacked out.

Her voice sounded far away as she told William to open the door, and then Riley realized she was carrying him into the kitchen. He had been too big to carry like that for years and he wondered how she could do it. He was breathing OK now and he slid his arms around her neck and kissed her cheek.

She set him down in a chair and stood beside him, still worried, as he looked around. The boys were there with the twins, who had followed everyone in.

"What happened?" asked Sam.

"I fell out of the tree," Riley explained. "Mom slapped my back and I couldn't breathe. Then she shook me and I couldn't breathe and here we are."

Mom looked funny, like she couldn't decide whether to laugh or cry. Then she laughed and laughed until tears ran down her cheeks and they all had to laugh with her.

"I thought I was helping," she finally said. "I did everything wrong, but it turned out all right, anyway, thank God! You sit there a minute. I'm going upstairs to get some disinfectant for your arm. We have to hurry because I want supper ready when Dad gets home." She kissed Riley lightly on the top of his head and ran up the back stairs.

Everyone spoke at once and then stopped at once, except for Jonathan, who said in a loud voice, "What's a Bahá'í Feast?"

William tried to explain. "In Manhattan, we have nine people called the Local Spiritual Assembly. They run the Bahá'í community and host the Feast, where everyone comes to the Bahá'í Center to read prayers and things. Sometimes we sing. The grownups talk a lot about what they call 'community administration' and we eat cookies and good stuff."

Riley nodded and added, "It's from the Bahá'í calendar. Since we are the only Bahá'ís in the area, we only do Feast by saying prayers together. And we eat dessert!"

"Can I come?" asked Jonathan. "I like good stuff to eat."

"We do, too," the girls said.

"Sure," said William. "We'll tell Mom. But keep the secret."

Together, Pam and Sam asked, "How do you know the secret?"

Riley said proudly, "There are two secrets and I'm the only one who knows both of them!" Then he closed his mouth tightly and made a zipping motion across his lips to show he wouldn't say anything more.

"Naw, I'll bet there's only one secret," said Jonathan, trying to get Riley to talk. Riley just shook his head and said nothing.

Mom rushed downstairs. While she cleaned the scrape on Riley's arm and covered it with a bandage, William said, "I told Jonathan they can come to Feast tonight. They can, can't they?"

Mom nodded and said to the Miller children. "I'll phone your mother now, and we'll see you after supper."

As they left, Jonathan whispered to Riley so no one else could hear, "I'm going to find out my sisters' secret. I'll make you tell me."

Riley's eyes grew wide. He wondered what Jonathan might do to him, but he shook his head. He wasn't going to tell Pam and Sam's secret to anyone!

Chapter Five

A SECRET CAN BE HARD TO KEEP

"Riley, slow down," said Dad in a kind tone of voice, as they sat around the kitchen table eating supper.

Riley felt as hungry as a wolf, maybe even two wolves! Still, he took the next bite of spaghetti more slowly. Loading the fork with as much as it could hold, he shoved it into his mouth, sucked in the strands that stuck out, and licked the sauce from his lips.

William was eating almost as fast, yet Mom only told him to eat some tossed salad, too. William didn't like vegetables, but Riley liked everything. Well, almost everything. He didn't like fish food. He had tasted it in kindergarten when he was feeding the pet fish. It was yucky.

Now Mom and Dad were talking about their work. Although they had moved to Hartland only a few days before, Dad was already driving to Columbus to teach summer school at the university. He told them about his new teaching job and then he told them that he had also gotten a consulting job. Business people often hired Dad to help them solve hard problems so they could make more money. Riley thought he might like to do that when he grew up, if he didn't work in the circus with Pam and Sam.

Mom said that she was having trouble doing her part-time job at home for a publishing company in New York City. People at the publisher's office sent her a book over the internet. On her computer, she fixed mistakes in it. Now she was supposed to send it back, but her computer wouldn't send it.

Dad said, "I'll see what I can do about it later. Right now, we need to get ready for Feast. This will be our first time having a Nineteen Day Feast in our new home. We're the only Bahá'ís in Hartland. It will be just us."

Mom said, "Not exactly. The boys invited the Miller children. I phoned their mom, Joy, to arrange it. She said her husband, Steve, is home from his sales trip. He wants to meet us and they will all be happy to come."

"That's great," said Dad. "We've been talking about finding people who want to know about the Faith, and maybe the Millers will have questions. We'll see."

After supper, Mom worked in the kitchen while Riley put cushions on the living room floor for the kids to sit on. Dad and William went upstairs to find some Bahá'í books for Feast. They would choose prayers and other things for people to read.

Soon Riley finished his job and went into the kitchen. Mom was humming as she put away the last of the clean supper dishes. When she took down a homemade cake from the top of the refrigerator, she let him carry it to the table all by himself. He accidentally stuck his thumbs into the chocolate frosting as he put it down. She used her clean fingers to smooth over the holes and they grinned at each other while they licked their fingers. After washing their hands again, they set out plates of crackers with cheese and plates of cut up fruit. Then they went into the living room.

Dad had brought home a surprise gift of flowers. With a smile, Mom sniffed them before he put the vase on the fireplace mantel beside the photograph of 'Abdu'l-Bahá. Riley knew that 'Abdu'l-Bahá had shown the Bahá'ís how to live what Bahá'u'lláh taught, especially about things called virtues, like friendliness, honesty, and kindness. He also knew that 'Abdu'l-Bahá was Bahá'u'lláh's son. What he didn't know was how a son could be old and have a white beard, but there was no time to think about it now.

Mom had chosen some music to play and started the CD player. A Bahá'í chorus was singing "We are all the waves of one sea, and the leaves of one tree, and the flowers of one garden" when the Millers arrived.

Dad welcomed them as they came in, talking and laughing. Jonathan said politely to Mom, "Excuse me. Could Riley show me where the bathroom is?" Riley led the way to the bathroom, and soon found himself alone upstairs with Jonathan.

Jonathan didn't waste any time. "Listen," he said in a low voice. "If you tell me my sisters' secret, I'll give you my bike."

Riley's eyes widened in surprise. "You'll give me your bike!" he exclaimed. He imagined himself riding it, with Jonathan scooting his scooter beside him, and William running way behind, unable to keep up. He smiled.

"Sure," said Jonathan. "Why not?"

Riley opened his mouth to say that it was only a dog hidden in the carriage shed. But then he thought of Sam and Pam, and how much fun he had with them and how he might join the circus with them some day, and no words came out.

Jonathan said, "Just tell me. No one will know. If you don't, you'll be sorry."

Riley didn't want to be sorry. He took another breath, and was almost about to tell him when, at that very moment, Dad called up to them that it was time to start, so they had to go downstairs. Riley breathed a big sigh of relief instead of telling.

They went downstairs and sat on the cushions that Riley had laid out. The music was playing quietly so that everyone sitting in the living room could hear Mom say, "Welcome to the Feast of Kalimát. Kalimát means 'words.' Words in the Bahá'í writings and other holy books tell us about God."

While the music continued softly, Jonathan read a children's prayer: "O God, guide me, protect me, make of me a shining lamp and a brilliant star. Thou art the Mighty and the Powerful." Then the adults took turns reading passages out loud from the Bahá'í books. Riley heard three words that he wondered about—paradise, reward, and punishment. But mostly he thought about his problem.

He really wanted the bike. Also, he really wanted to be friends with Sam and Pam, and he felt sure that they wouldn't want to be his friends if he told. Yet Jonathan had said that Riley would be sorry if he didn't tell. What did Jonathan mean?

Soon, Dad turned off the CD player and asked William and Riley to stand with him and Mom to sing a prayer to close the devotional part of Feast. They sang, "Is there any Remover of difficulties save God? Say: Praised be God! He is God! All are His servants, and all abide by His bidding!" Riley sang with all his heart. Not only did he love to sing, but he had a real difficulty.

After they finished singing, there was a moment of quiet. Then Mom said, "We have refreshments in the kitchen, but first, how about a story for the children?" And all Riley's worries went right out of his head because listening to Mom tell a story was one of the things he liked best in the whole world.

Chapter Six

THINGS ARE DIFFERENT THAN THEY SEEM

"Once upon a time," Mom began the story, "there was a great and wise king who had a son. This boy was about your age."

"My age?" asked William.

Mom pointed at him and said, "Yes!" Then she laughed and pointed at each person and said "Yes." They all laughed, too, and she continued. "This boy had heard of a place with two names. Sometimes it was called paradise and sometimes heaven. Whatever it was called, he longed to visit it. He wanted to see for himself what it was like.

"So one day he said, 'O great king who is my father, please allow this servant who is your son, the prince, to visit heaven.' Or maybe what he said was, 'Hey, King Dad, can I go take a look at paradise?'

"The great and wise king answered, 'My son, I have always intended for you to know paradise. This is my command to you. You must go forth to find it, never giving up, no matter what the

difficulties.' And he added, 'There is one and only one way to get there.' Or maybe what he said was, 'Sure, son. Listen while I tell you the way.'

"So the prince asked, 'How do I get there?'

"And the mighty king answered, 'By bicycle.'

"'By bicycle!' exclaimed the prince. He had expected to dress in armor and gallop away upon a great white pony, or at least to zoom off in a miniature sports car.

"'Yes,' said the king, and he gave his son the gift of a very fancy bicycle. The bicycle was a Silver Gleamer Streamer with handlebars of gold, but to tell you the truth, any old bicycle would have done just as well.

"So the prince said, 'Many thanks, O king, who is the most generous of fathers.' Or maybe what he said was, 'Hey, King Dad, that bike is way cool!'

"Now the first thing the boy had to do was learn to ride the bicycle. That wasn't easy." Mom looked at William and then at Riley. Riley shifted uneasily as he sat cross-legged on the floor cushion. He wondered if she somehow knew what had happened that afternoon. But she went on with the story.

"He had many adventures until one day, he came to a sign where roads crossed each other. He was happy to see this sign, for on it, printed in big black and white letters—or maybe in flashing pink neon—was the word 'Paradise.'

"Now this was a very strange sign. Instead of one arrow pointing in one direction, it had six arrows. One pointed to the East, one to the West, one to the North, one to the South and, hmm, where did the other two arrows point?"

William squirmed and blurted, "I know! They pointed to in-between roads." Mom shook her head as she said, "A good guess, but there were only four roads." No one else had a guess, so she continued. "I told you it was a very strange sign. One of the other two arrows pointed up and the other pointed down."

The twins spoke together. They said, "But you can't ride a bicycle," and Sam finished with "up" while Pam finished with "down." Then they looked at each other and giggled so hard that everyone else had to laugh, too.

Mom said, "The prince wondered about that as well. He didn't know what to do, so he got off the bike, stuck out his pointer finger like this, and turned around." All the kids jumped up and turned around with their eyes shut and their pointer fingers stuck out. She said, "And when he stopped . . ." Everyone stopped and sat down again, except William. Dad reached out and pulled him onto his lap.

"And when he stopped," Mom repeated, "he went where the finger pointed. He had gone almost no distance at all when he and the bike fell. This happened now and then because he was a new rider. He hit his head and blacked out."

Riley knew what that felt like. He hadn't hit his head, but when he fell from the tree and couldn't get his breath, he had blacked out. He listened intently, wondering what would happen next.

Mom said, "When he opened his eyes, he saw the most amazing thing. He was at home and there was his father. But somehow home was brighter and more beautiful than he had ever seen it and his father was so magnificent that the boy could barely look at him. 'My Lord,' he said, and got up and knelt at his father's feet, or maybe he just knelt and said softly, 'Wow! Awesome!'

"And the great king said to him, raising him up, 'My child, whoever follows my commands arrives at the paradise of my good pleasure.' Or maybe what he said was, 'Son, you get to heaven by obedience to my commands.'"

Then Mom smiled, made a silly bow, and sat down.

Everyone clapped and William said, "I wish I had a Silver Gleamer Streamer!"

Joy Miller looked at her husband, Steve. He nodded at her. She said, "William, Jonathan has something to tell you. Go ahead, Jonathan."

Jonathan stared at the floor, looking uncomfortable. Then he said in a low voice, "My bike's too small. I'm getting a new big one. You can have my old one."

William was so excited that he leaped from Dad's lap and jumped up and down. As Dad asked, "What about saying thank you?" Riley heard Mom whisper to Mrs. Miller, "That's very generous, but Jonathan doesn't look happy about it."

"He was before," Joy whispered back.

Riley's mouth had dropped open in surprise. Jonathan had

known all the time that the bike was going to William! Riley felt very relieved that he had not told the secret.

Jonathan wouldn't look at him when Mom had the kids sit at the kitchen table for refreshments. The adults stood around them, holding their plates as they ate and talked.

Steve Miller asked, "Do you have Feasts often?"

Mom replied, "The Bahá'í Faith has a different calendar. A year is still a year, but we have nineteen months instead of twelve. The first day of each month is a Feast day. So, kids, how many Feast days are there?"

"Nineteen," shouted the kids, except for Riley, who had his mouth full of chocolate cake.

Dad asked, "How many days are there in a regular year?"

Jonathan said, "Three hundred and sixty-five. I learned that when I was little."

"Good," said Dad, smiling. "But nineteen months of nineteen days gives us only 361 days. Guess what we do with the other days."

William couldn't wait for them to guess. "Presents, parties!" he shouted.

Mom said, "Let's use our indoor voices." And then she said, "These days have two names. They're called Intercalary Days or Ayyám-i-Há."

"Wow!" said Jonathan. "It's like you have Christmas for four days instead of one." He told his parents, "I want to be Bahá'í, too!"

The adults laughed, and Mom said, "There's a lot more to it than that. We're going to have children's classes soon. Maybe you can come. We learn about all religions."

Steve and Joy Miller asked so many questions that soon the grownups took their refreshments into the living room so that they could sit down to talk. As they left the kitchen, Dad asked William to bring down more Bahá'í books from their bedroom and William ran up the back stairs.

Jonathan said to his sisters, "Riley told me your secret."

Forgetting his indoor voice, Riley shouted, "I did not!"

Jonathan said, "Well, you were going to, but we had to go downstairs."

Pam glared at Riley, while Sam looked upset.

Riley explained, "I didn't tell, but I did want the bike."

"What bike?" demanded Pam.

Riley answered, "Jonathan told me that I could have his bike if I told."

Jonathan said to Riley, "I was joking. You're too little to know when someone's joking."

"I am not!" exclaimed Riley. "I'm glad I didn't tell you. I'll never tell you!"

"You better not," said Pam, but Sam looked away. She still wouldn't look at him or talk to him when everyone was saying good night as they were leaving. He kept watching her sadly, hoping she would say something.

However, when the Millers left, it was Jonathan who spoke. He whispered quietly to Riley as he walked out the door, "I told you that you'd be sorry."

Chapter Seven

THE BEST THING TO DO

The second Riley woke up the next morning, he jumped out of bed. He could hardly wait to slip out to the carriage shed to visit the dog. He pulled on his t-shirt and jeans, pushed his bare feet into his sneakers, splashed water on his face, combed his hair with his hands, and ran down the back stairs.

Mom, Dad, and William were already eating at the kitchen table.

"Here he is," said Mom as Riley sat down. She kissed the top of his head on her way to the stove to get his plate of food. "We let you sleep late."

"I thought you would be at work," Riley said to his father, and then took his first big bites of scrambled eggs and toast.

Dad said, "I don't have to teach today, so I decided to do something special with you and William. We need a place to keep the car, so we're going to clean out the carriage shed."

At hearing that, Riley jumped and accidentally knocked over his glass of orange juice, spilling some of it on his shirt and the rest on the floor.

"Oh my goodness!" exclaimed Mom. She brought wet and dry towels over to where Riley was sitting, and they cleaned up the sticky mess together. "This will do for now," she said, "but you'll have to change your clothes when you're done eating."

"OK," said Riley in a small voice. If they cleaned out the carriage shed, Dad and William would discover the dog, and how would Sam and Pam know that he hadn't told their secret? This was terrible. He wanted to say a prayer for help right then, but he couldn't. He had to eat.

"By the way, Riley," Mom said, "when I was putting your jeans into the washing machine, I found this in your pocket." She laid a wrinkled piece of paper on the table.

Riley stared at the paper that he had picked up yesterday after he fell with the bike. He had forgotten about it. "What does it say?" he asked.

Mom answered, "It seems to be a notice for a lost dog."

Dad pointed and said, "Yes. This looks like the word 'lost,' except the letter 'l' is missing. And here is a picture of the front half of a bulldog."

Mom added, "And the whole phone number is here at the bottom of the page so we can call if we see it."

Riley looked at William, worried that his brother would guess that the dog was his secret. However, William had made a train from his toast crusts. He was moving them around his plate, muttering to himself, "Chug-chug-chug, woo-woo!"

After breakfast, Mom kept William with her to help with dishes and sent Riley upstairs to change his clothes. As he ran up the back stairs, all he could think of was the prayer he was already saying. He didn't even hear the telephone ring.

When he came back downstairs a few minutes later, he was very surprised to find that no one was there except his mother. His heart thudded in alarm. Dad and William must have already gone out to the carriage shed.

Mom turned from the sink, where she was finishing the dishes. "You can dry if you're careful," she said, handing him a towel.

"I thought William was helping," said Riley.

"He had to go with Dad," Mom explained. Seeing the look on his face, she added, "Oh dear! Dad said he didn't think you would mind. The sooner they left, the sooner they would get back so you can all work on the carriage shed."

Riley's face brightened. It looked like God was answering his prayer already. "Where are they?" he asked.

"Mrs. Miller had a flat tire after she dropped her kids off for their music lessons. She couldn't get the tire off because the nuts were on the bolts so tightly. Mr. Miller left early this morning on another business trip, so she asked Dad to come and help her."

"Good!" exclaimed Riley.

"What's good?" asked Mom, jokingly. "Her having a flat tire or Dad's helpfulness?"

"God is good," Riley said, "I asked for something and I got it really fast."

Mom, still joking, said, "Did you pray for Mrs. Miller to have a flat tire?"

"No," said Riley. He decided he better not say anything else in case he said too much. He felt uncomfortable. He liked keeping a secret from William, but it felt strange to be keeping secrets from Mom.

Mom handed him a plate to dry. She looked thoughtful as she rinsed some dishes. Soon, she said, "Of course God can give us what we ask for really fast. But prayer isn't like putting a coin into a candy machine, pressing a button, and out pops what you want."

Riley laughed and said, "I know that! Can I go outdoors after dishes?"

Mom was surprised and pleased. Unless Riley was with the older boys, he usually wanted to play with the electronic game machine and other toys, or look at *Brilliant Star* magazine, or pretend to read books. "Yes," she said. "Run along now. I'll finish."

He threw the dish towel onto the drainer, gave Mom a quick hug, and ran outside.

The carriage shed had double front doors big enough to drive a horse and carriage or a car through. They were too heavy for Riley to open, so he went in the side door. He could hear the dog crying. She didn't sound unhappy or lonesome. She sounded hurt.

The noise came from the other side of the shed. He hurried toward it, dodging around things that had been left on the dusty wood floor where the horses used to stand to be hitched to carriages or wagons. Then he came to the row of box stalls, where the horses used to live. The door to each stall had a top and a bottom. When the top was open, the horse could look out but not get out. Riley followed the sounds to the middle stall, where the top half of the door was open.

"I'm coming," he told the dog as he grabbed the door latch, but it wouldn't open. He put his hands on the top of the door and tried to pull himself up to see over it, but he couldn't quite do it. The dog cried louder and tried to dig her way through the door to get to him.

"I have to see what's wrong with you," he said. He looked around for something to stand on. A heavy ladder like a steep staircase went up to the loft, where hay had been kept to feed the horses. If Riley climbed up the ladder and looked down, he knew he would be able to see the dog. But the last time he had climbed a ladder, he had fallen.

The dog began to bark frantically.

"Sh!" he hissed. "We don't want anyone to hear you!"

She just barked louder. Then she yelped and made a scrambling noise. Suddenly, there was a thump as if she had fallen, and she was quiet except for making some huffing and low moaning noises.

Riley climbed up the ladder as carefully as he could. When he glanced down to make sure the floor wasn't getting too far away, he felt relieved because in a couple more steps he would be able to see the dog.

She was lying down close to the stall door. Suddenly, she gave another sharp yelp and lurched to her feet. She tried to bite one of her sides, then the other. Of course she couldn't, but she did step in the dish the twins had left for her, and that upended, flinging water everywhere. Any other time, Riley would have laughed, but he didn't feel like laughing now. Quickly, still being careful, he backed down the ladder.

When he reached the floor, he ran back to the stall and stuck his fingers through a knot hole. As she licked them, he said, "I can't see what's wrong. I have to go get my Mom. She knows how to make hurts stop. It's the best thing to do."

Chapter Eight

"HELLO! THIS IS AN EMERGENCY!"

Riley ran to the house as fast as he could. He could still hear the dog crying and barking. He didn't want to break his promise to the twins, but it sounded as though the dog was really hurt so he had to get help.

"Mom! Mom!" Riley shouted as he burst into the kitchen. No answer. He ran through the dining room, living room, and hallway calling her, but she wasn't there. He ran upstairs, still calling. She wasn't there, either. Where could she be? She had never left him alone without saying where she was going. What should he do?

He ran back to the kitchen. The idea of praying came into his mind and left it just as fast. He wanted Dad. He wanted Dad right this minute because he knew Dad would be able to help. But Dad wasn't there, either.

Riley wondered what Dad would do. Well, first he would say what he always said: "There are lots of ways to solve a problem.

What are some of your choices?" So Riley looked around the kitchen.

"This is an emergency," he said to himself. "In an emergency you dial 9-1-1 for help." Mom had hung a telephone on the kitchen wall because she didn't want to hunt for it, and Riley could reach it when he climbed onto a chair. Although he had used a phone to talk to Granny and Grandpa, he had never pushed the buttons to make the call. He studied the numbers. Now, which was the six and which was the nine?

Suddenly he heard footsteps coming up the stairs from the basement. It was Mom! She had been downstairs taking clothes out of the dryer and she looked very surprised to see Riley with the phone in his hand.

"She's hurt," Riley explained. "I wanted to call for help."

"Who's hurt?" asked Mom, hurrying over to him.

"The dog in the carriage shed," he said. "She must be hurt because she keeps barking and whining and I didn't know what to do and I couldn't find you."

"Uh oh!" exclaimed Mom. She put the clothes she was carrying onto the counter and swung Riley down from the chair. Holding hands, they ran to the carriage shed. Mom was tall enough to see over the top of the stall door.

"Oh my goodness!" she almost shouted. The dog was excited and she woofed and huffed and whined, ending with a sharp yelp of pain.

Mom couldn't stop saying, "Oh my goodness!" She let go of Riley's hand and ran back to the house so fast that he couldn't keep up.

She dialed the number on the notice for the lost dog. Her hand shook and she repeated, "Be there! Be there! Be there!" Suddenly she said, "Hello? Hello! This is an emergency. I think we found your lost dog and it looks like she needs help!"

After talking to the dog's owner briefly, Mom hung up the phone. "Thank God the owner answered," she said to Riley. "She's calling the vet first and then she'll come over as fast as she can. It looks like the bulldog is about to give birth and needs some help from a veterinarian. She said that sometimes bulldogs can die if they don't have a vet to help them when their puppies are born."

Riley's eyes widened. "Is she going to die?" he asked.

Mom gave him a quick hug. "Her chance of surviving just got a whole lot better. Let's go stay with her while we're waiting."

They hurried back to the carriage shed. The dog was barking softly with low, huffy woofs. As they arrived, her voice rose in sharp cries of pain. Mom managed to get the stall door open, and Riley went in with her.

"Hey, Cleopatra," Mom said quietly, having learned the dog's name from the owner, as she knelt down and began to pet her gently. The dog was sitting with her front legs wide, as if she were having trouble holding herself up. However, she licked the hand Mom held out.

"God loves animals, too, and we're going to pray for you," Mom continued. "Riley, why don't you say a prayer and then I'll say one."

Riley nodded, and took his turn. Then Mom sang, "Say: God sufficeth all things above all things, and nothing in the heavens or in the earth but God sufficeth. Verily, He is in Himself the Knower, the Sustainer, the Omnipotent."

Riley felt relieved that Mom was saying this prayer. "Sufficeth" was hard for him to say, although he knew it meant that God can meet every need.

He didn't know how many turns he and Mom had taken saying prayers when everything happened at once. Suddenly Cleopatra seemed to be doing a duet with the wailing siren of a police car. Then the siren stopped, and they heard people getting out of cars and talking loudly. Mom jumped up and rushed outside to see what was happening. She quickly came back with a scowling white-haired woman, who was carrying a heavy blanket. Closely at the woman's heels followed an unhappy police officer.

"Where's my girl?" shouted the woman. Before anyone could answer, she barged into the stall and threw the blanket down beside the dog. Cleopatra got up to greet her, trying to wag her stubby tail, and ended up yelping in pain.

"My poor doggie!" the woman crooned, spread the blanket, and very gently urged Cleopatra onto it. Cleopatra kept whining and crying. The sound made Riley want to cry, too, but he didn't.

"Make yourself useful," the woman snapped at the police officer, who was standing near the stall door by Mom. "Try to pull me over for speeding, will you, young man? I knew you when you wore diapers." Riley imagined the grownup police officer wearing nothing but diapers. It was a funny idea, but Riley didn't feel like laughing.

The woman told the policeman, "Pick up that side of the blanket and we'll carry her to my van. The vet should be ready by the time we get there."

Cleopatra was heavy, but the two adults managed to carry her between them in the blanket. Mom ran ahead of them to open the side door of the woman's van. They placed Cleopatra as gently as possible on the floor of the van and she stopped crying.

The woman said to Mom, "Bless you for being so helpful! Will you ride in back with her while I drive and the police car goes ahead of us?"

Mom nodded and asked, "What about Riley?" All three adults looked at him. Right then Joy Miller drove into her driveway next door with a hello honk of the horn and she and her three kids looked at him, too. After her came William with Dad, who parked behind the police car. Suddenly it felt to Riley like the whole world was looking at him.

Dad and William jumped out of their car and rushed over to them. Dad asked, "What's going on here?"

Mom was climbing into the van. "I have to go help out, but Riley will tell you," she said, and closed the door. "Everything's going to be OK," they heard her croon to the dog, who had started to cry again. The policeman leaped into his car, turned on his siren, and both vehicles sped away.

Joy came over to Dad, followed by all three of her children. "What on earth is happening?" she exclaimed.

Dad replied, "That's what I want to know. And Riley is about to tell us."

Chapter Nine

REWARD AND PUNISHMENT

Riley looked down at the ground. Everyone was staring at him. Everyone knew he told the secret. The sound of the dog's yelps of pain was still in his ears and he didn't see how she could hurt so much and not die. He felt like crying himself.

Without looking up, he said, "I did it." He could hardly get the words out.

Dad hunkered down in front of him. "Look at me, Riley," he said quietly. "What did you do?"

When Riley looked in his father's face, he found that he could talk. "I told. The dog was in the carriage shed. She got hurt, so I told Mom."

Dad asked gently, "How did the dog get hurt?"

Riley wasn't sure how to answer the question because he wasn't exactly sure how the dog got hurt. Finally he said, "She's having puppies!"

Jonathan shouted. "That's it! That's the secret!" He said to his sisters, "You found that dog and hid her. I told you I'd find out."

Now everyone looked at the twins.

The twins looked at each other, and then Pam turned to her mom and said loudly, "I wanted a bulldog puppy and I still want one!"

Joy Miller made a disapproving mother noise, grabbed Pam by the arm and marched her toward their house. Over her shoulder, she called back to Dad, "Talk with you later," and to her other children she said, "Come on."

Instead of following his mom, Jonathan ran to the carriage shed with William at his heels. Dad went, too, holding Riley's hand. Sam trailed behind. One quick glance back at her face told Riley that she felt extremely unhappy.

Jonathan and William were already in the stall. "Oh!" Jonathan exclaimed as William shouted, "Look at that!" Big and little spots of blood had turned dark and soaked into the old wood floor.

Riley said, "She started bleeding sometimes when she moved. Dad, will she die?"

"I can't say," Dad replied. "I hope not. Everything's being done for her that can be done, thanks to you."

Riley still felt miserable but he liked what Dad said. He wondered what Sam thought about it. To his dismay, he saw tears running down her cheeks.

Jonathan started to tease her, but Dad said, "Your mother told you to go home. Do it." Jonathan looked surprised, but he went, with William still at his heels.

Sam didn't move. Dad hunkered down in front of her like he had with Riley, so their eyes met. "Do you want to talk about it?" he asked.

She said, "Pam wanted a puppy so bad. We didn't know this would happen."

Riley asked, "Are you mad at me?"

She blinked away her tears, sniffed hard, and said, "No, you had to tell."

Dad said, "Sam, do you understand that hiding the dog was wrong?"

"But Pam wanted a puppy!" she protested.

"It was still wrong. When you found the dog, you should have told your parents so they could try to find the owner. You know that, don't you?"

Sam looked into Dad's eyes. Then she nodded.

"Good," Dad said. "I hope you'll do better next time. Will you try?"

Sam asked carefully, "What will next time be?"

Dad chuckled and said, "I don't know. When you find out, you can tell me! Will you try?"

Sam thought it over. When she said, "OK," Riley knew she meant it and so did Dad. Dad smiled and stood up.

Riley said in a small voice, "Dad, I broke a promise. I wasn't supposed to tell anyone the secret."

It was Dad's turn to look thoughtful. Finally, he said, "That's a tough one. Bahá'u'lláh wants Bahá'ís to do what they say they'll do. But we shouldn't make promises about something we know is wrong. Since we need to be careful about the promises we make, how about consulting with your mother or me first?"

Riley knew that consulting meant talking things over. Being told he could consult with his parents made him feel very grown up, so he said, "OK."

"Now, Sam . . ." Dad said, but she interrupted him.

"I know," she said. "My mom wanted me to go home. Bye!" And she turned around and ran out the door.

Dad closed the stall and carriage shed doors and he and Riley walked back to the house. On the way, his cell phone rang. What Riley could hear him say didn't make much sense. Finally Dad said, "Good, we'll see you later," and clicked off the phone.

Then he told Riley, "Mom says things are OK. Cleopatra is having surgery now and Mom is waiting with the owner. And Mom said Cleopatra's owner wants everyone to call her Mamaw."

"Mamaw? What kind of a name is that?" asked Riley.

Dad said, "She told Mom that it's what everyone calls her. It's like calling her Nana or Grandma." Laughing, he added, "Cleopatra is named after a beautiful queen of ancient Egypt because Mamaw thinks that funny-looking dog is beautiful!"

Surprised, Riley said, "But she is beautiful!" Dad laughed harder, so Riley added, "At least when she smiles."

Dad reached down and ruffled Riley's hair affectionately. "I guess it all depends on your point of view, doesn't it?" he said.

Riley nodded and, as they went into the kitchen together, Dad's phone rang again. This time it was Joy Miller. William had told her about the plan to clean up the carriage shed. She wanted to thank Dad for helping her change the flat tire on her car by offering to help with the work in the carriage shed. Dad invited her to bring her children over and eat lunch first.

By the time they had all crowded into the kitchen and made sandwiches, cut up some carrots and celery, washed apples, and poured milk, it was almost noon. They sat around the kitchen table and ate and talked. Riley liked the strawberry jam on his peanut butter sandwich. In fact, he liked it so much that he decided to have it for dessert and stuck his fingers into the jam jar for more, but Dad saw what he was doing and said that was enough. When they all washed dishes afterward and put things away, Dad had him wash his hands with soap and water so he wouldn't stick to everything he touched. Then they all went out to the carriage shed.

Dad said, "We want to use this for the garage. The goal is to clear the junk away so that we can drive the car in through the big doors and park it." He showed everyone where to put trash to be thrown out, and where to stack things to be taken care of later.

After awhile, the girls went up the ladder to explore the hay loft. Riley could hear them talking while he carried things to Dad for him to decide what to keep and what to throw out. Time went by very slowly but he felt relieved to have something to do while he waited to find out about Cleopatra and her puppies.

At last, the van returned with its horn honking. Everyone rushed out to meet Mom and the woman called "Mamaw" as they got out of the vehicle.

Riley flung his arms around Mom where she stood on the lawn, and asked, "Is she OK? Are the puppies OK?"

"Yes and yes," Mom said, hugging him back.

Mamaw looked at the twins and they moved closer together. "You're the ones who hid my Cleopatra," she said sternly. Then she said to Riley, "And you're the one who saved her life."

Riley said, "I told my mom." There didn't seem to be anything else to say.

The woman stared at him for a moment. Then she suddenly smiled and said, "I want you to have a reward for doing the right thing. Would you like to have one of Cleopatra's puppies?"

Riley's mouth formed an "O" of surprise. This wasn't happening to William first, the way things usually did. This was happening to him. "Yes!" he shouted. Then he added to Dad and Mom, "Can I?" Dad nodded and Mom grinned.

Riley barely remembered to say thank you. He tried to listen to what Mamaw was saying about how the puppy had to grow up some first, and to Dad about how it was a big job to take care of a dog. Yet he couldn't help thinking about finding Cleopatra in the woods. He had wanted her to like him best. However, he soon saw that she loved everybody. That was OK, he guessed. But somehow he knew that he and his puppy were going to be extra special to each other.

Then he did listen, because Joy Miller said, "When my husband gets home from his sales trip, we'll think of a punishment for the girls."

Mamaw spoke to the twins, mostly to Pam. "If you had done the right thing, I would have given you the puppy." Pam started crying, turned, and ran toward her house. Mamaw continued, now talking to Mrs. Miller. "When you don't get what you want and somebody else does, that can often be punishment enough."

Mrs. Miller nodded in agreement. "Yes, I believe you're right."

The adults began to talk. The older boys pretended they didn't care that it was Riley who was getting a dog and went off to play. Riley followed Sam as she started walking back home to be with Pam. He felt delighted about the puppy, yet sad for the twins. It was hard for him to have two strong feelings at the same time.

Suddenly, Sam turned to him and said, "If we can't have the puppy, I'm glad you can." Then she ran into her house, the screen door slamming shut behind her.

Now Riley felt only one way. He was completely happy. And as he went home to his new old house, he had a wonderful idea. He would let Pam and Sam play with his puppy whenever they wanted. That way they would be happy, too!

THE END

BAHÁ'Í PUBLISHING AND THE BAHÁ'Í FAITH

Bahá'í Publishing produces books based on the teachings of the Bahá'í Faith. Founded over 160 years ago, the Bahá'í Faith has spread to some 235 nations and territories and is now accepted by more than five million people. The word "Bahá'í" means "follower of Bahá'u'lláh." Bahá'u'lláh, the founder of the Bahá'í Faith, asserted that He is the Messenger of God for all of humanity in this day. The cornerstone of His teachings is the establishment of the spiritual unity of humankind, which will be achieved by personal transformation and the application of clearly identified spiritual principles. Bahá'ís also believe that there is but one religion and that all the Messengers of God—among them Abraham, Zoroaster, Moses, Krishna, Buddha, Jesus, and Muhammad—have progressively revealed its nature. Together, the world's great religions are expressions of a single, unfolding divine plan. Human beings, not God's Messengers, are the source of religious divisions, prejudices, and hatreds.

The Bahá'í Faith is not a sect or denomination of another religion, nor is it a cult or a social movement. Rather, it is a globally recognized independent world religion founded on new books of scripture revealed by Bahá'u'lláh.

Bahá'í Publishing is an imprint of the National Spiritual Assembly of the Bahá'ís of the United States.